JOHN VALLES

ROLY-POLY MARY SLIMSHIP

AND THE

BAG OF QUARTERS

aheadonthetablestory

Chapter One

Welcome to Dipdrought

It was the monthly dance and bash in Dipdrought Oregon. Little Roly-Poly Mary Slimship stared across the dance floor and hardly could believe her eyes. "A bag of Quarters!" she almost gasped out loud, and sure enough it was. Mary noticed that none of the other girls had gotten up the nerve to make a move and she wasn't surprised. Dipdrought had rarely seen a bag of quarters, nickels maybe, but never quarters. "If only," she thought. Dare she even dream? Mary's 5'2" frame was as big around as she was tall, and she was looking quite fetching in her, newly purchased, steamed broccoli colored jumpsuit and brown leather clogs. She pulled a mirror out of her purse and ran her fingers through her short crop of red, blondish, charcoal streaked hair. Then she pinched her pale, freckled cheeks and started gliding gracefully around the room, well, as gracefully as a roly-poly in high-heeled brown leather clogs could, that is.

Mary stopped a few feet away from the object her desire. He was standing by the refreshment table. She scooped up a glass of punch and sidled up to him. He was beautiful. He stood a full six feet tall at least, had thinning, dusky blond hair and, oh, the most interesting face she had ever seen. He looked as if someone had taken a bag of about a thousand quarters and pelted him, mercilessly in the face with them, one by one, and to top off the alluring package, his head looked as if it had taken a few baseball bat blows. Craters and pock-marks blanketed his face and balding head. Not smooth craters, like a with a bag of nickels, but rough, ragged craters. Oil and dirt pockets. Perfect breeding grounds for blackheads. Mary swooned thinking about the hours she could spend just staring into those crevices in search of new blackheads and she dreamed of sitting a coffee cup in the crater sized indentation on the right side of his head while he rested it on her lap. Well, she didn't actually have a lap, but, still, she could dream.

Mary began to sway back forth to the music. She desperately wanted to talk to this man and was trying to think of a good opening line when, abruptly, she lost her balance and fell into him, spilling her red punch all over the both of them. "Oh my god, what an idiot", she thought to herself. She began to stammer out an apology but the bag of quarters cut her off, "It's O.K.", he assured her.

"I'll get some napkins from the table. I'm a complete moron", Mary said, mortified, "What must you think of me? "

"It's O.K.," the bag of quarters said again, "Accidents happen, and I have plenty more shirts back at my hotel room".

"Oh, and what hotel would that be?" Mary asked.

 "The "Coat and Arms," He replied.

"Of course, where else would such an interesting person be staying?" Mary said, as she wiped the punch from her outfit.

Mary was now in full fantasy mode. "How happy would mom be if I could bag this one?" she thought. Mary's sister, Alice, had always been criticized by their parents for wanting a mere beer belly type. "They're so common and uninteresting." Her mother would say "Especially for a girl with your malformations," and Mary had to agree, a crooked armed hunchback like Alice certainly could do much better.

Mary returned her attention to the bag of quarters. "I'm sorry if I seem pushy, but I can tell that you're not from around here and I was wondering if you might like some company. I understand if you don't, after all, you are such an interesting person and I'm just a common Roly-Poly. I'm not exactly a Hump, like my sister."

"Your sister is a Hump? That's hot. What side, right or left?"

"See, I knew it, and I might as well tell you that she has a gimpy arm and a club foot while I'm at it. What difference does it make anyway. If you did hang out with me it would probably just be so you could meet her. I've been down that road before."

"Believe me, Mary, gimpy-armed, club-footed Humps don't really do anything for me. I find you much more interesting."

"Sure." Mary said, "you're just saying that."

"Honestly", "I remember when I was a young boy, I had quite a huge crush on this roly-poly math teacher at my grammar school and you remind me of her an awful lot."

Mary's first instincts told her that she was being led on, that she was being lied to and should probably just keep the conversation casual and not pursue this person because something didn't seem quite right. So, she squelched those horrible thoughts and let her emotions take over. "Well, let me introduce myself," she said, extending a pudgy hand, "I'm Mary Slimship."

"Pleased to meet you," the bag of quarters replied, "I'm Patrick Hatrick. So, tell me something about yourself, Mary, are you from Dipdrought or did you just drive up here for the dance?"

"Yes, I'm from Dipdrought. I live here with my parents and my sister, Alice."

"So, tell me a little more about your family. I'll bet that they're all really interesting people."

"Well, I already told you about my sister, Alice, but besides that, she just turned eighteen and is graduating high school this year, but, I mean, with her looks why even bother with school. I'm sure some guy will scoop her up in no time and take care of her for the rest of her life. My parents' names are Alec and Fannie. My Dad's a double-amp and my Mom's a leper." Mary added.

"Wow, that's pretty impressive, Mary."

"Thanks. He lost an arm and a foot to a farm accident when he was a boy, so, I mean, he wasn't exactly born that way," Mary said.

"Hey, sometimes God has to make up later for what he missed in the womb." Patrick said. And your Mom's a leper?"

"Yes, dad always told us that he had more to gain, by marrying her, then he had left to lose."

"Ha, ha, your dad has quite a sense of humor." Patrick laughed.

"Sure, but It's easy for him, he's such an interesting person. I envy them both so much. Sometimes I wish I could, at least, become an amp like my dad."

"Well that's not a bad thought, "Patrick told her, but don't do anything foolish, because you know that if it's intentional it doesn't count."

"I know, "Mary responded, "Not to mention that you'd be shamed for the rest of your life if people found out, or even suspected. So, tell me something about your family, Patrick."

"Well, I grew up in Oakland. My dad's an Adonis type and my mom's a palsy."

"Wow, how did he land her? Not that I'm putting him down," Mary added apologetically, "I would never, ever, do anything like that."

"I know what you meant, Mary, don't worry about it. I guess she just liked his personality, well that and the fact that he has a pretty high handicap in golf."

Mary broke into a fit of laughter. "You've got quite a sense of humor, yourself, Patrick," she said, still laughing.

"Well, Mary, some people are just easier to talk to than others," Patrick said, softly, gazing into Mary's eyes".

Mary swallowed hard, then made her play. 'I'd like to get to know you better, if you're going to be in town for a while." she said, hopefully.

"I think I'd like that too." Patrick replied, smiling.

Mary stood motionless, she couldn't believe that this was actually happening to her. At that same instant, she became aware of the stares she was getting from the other girls in the room. There was, the emaciated, Donna Harfacts, with her skeletal frame, pointy nose and crooked toothed overbite. There was Norma "Noodle" Baumgard, who had been born with no bones in her left arm, Amy Anthony Oralface, the hermaphrodite and all the others. The cream of Dipdrought, who had been saving themselves all of these years, waiting for their interesting prince to come along and carry them off to an interesting life. Waiting for someone like Patrick Hatrick, the bag of quarters. Mary felt like the luckiest girl in the world.

Chapter Two
Part One
Hulking Harry Humbleton

Hulking Harry Humbleton was a six foot 4 inch tall specimen of boring physical perfection. Throughout history his classic good looks had been done to death. The sandy blond hair, the high cheekbones, the finely chiseled muscles, puhleeease, could he be any more predictable? What had once been considered heartthrob material was now considered to be uninteresting and unremarkable, even repulsive.

In spite of Harry's physical disadvantages he was determined to make his mark. Harry had aspirations beyond the lowly job he now held as a delivery man for Jawbone's bakery and deli

Harry was working on an invention, an invention that he hoped would not only make him rich, but would also help him to win the heart of Mary Slimship, the girl he had loved secretly for years.

Alone in his basement apartment, Harry had just put the final touches on the fifth attempt at his invention and was ready to try it out. He plugged the cord into the wall and flipped the power switch to "on". Moments later the smell of burning wires stung his nostrils, a fuse blew and the lights went out. Harry sat in the dark for several seconds, "almost got it", he mumbled.

Chapter 2

Part Two
Meeting the Slimships

The mood was a happy one at the Slimship household. Mary insisted that Patrick come to her house after the dance and meet her family. They were all sitting around the parlor exchanging pleasantries.

"My, but you're an interesting person." Mary's mother, Fannie, was saying to Patrick.

"Not half as interesting as you" Patrick replied in such a charming manner that Fannie began to giggle.

"Would you like something to drink?" Mary's father, Alec, asked, "We've got some of that potato juice cocktail everybody's raving about. Have you tried it yet?"

The mention of the potato juice cocktail made Patrick cringe in fear for a moment, but he quickly regained his composure and hoped that no one had noticed his reaction. "No." Patrick replied, "I'm fine. Don't go to any trouble for my sake."

"Dad," Mary said excitedly, "Why don't you get your guitar and play a song? He's really good." She told Patrick. "He's been playing since high school, and he still plays gigs around town."

"Good idea." Alec said.

Patrick protested, but minutes later Alec returned with his guitar. He fingered the chords with his one remaining hand, while strumming the strings with his toes, and crooned out a lively rendition of "My Girl tis of Thee."

"If you're a good girl or a bad girl
I'll love you just the same
I'll eat you like a snack, girl
until you call my name

She may not seem like much to you
But to me she's everything
She is my girl tis of thee
And it's of her I sing"

Everybody joined in for the chorus, with an elated Mary, singing the loudest.

"Oh, my girl tis of thee
always so sweet to me
It's of thee I sing"

Patrick applauded. "The old songs always have the most meaning. Great job folks".

"Mom, tell Patrick the story about how you lost the little finger on your right hand." Mary said.

"Oh, he doesn't want to hear that." Her mother answered.

"Please, mom. It's so romantic." Mary pleaded.

"Alright, if you insist," Fannie said. "I lost that finger on the night that Mary's father asked me to marry him. I was in such a daze after he proposed that I forgot to check myself, as you know we lepers must since we lose feeling due to our disease, and any little cut can turn into a major infection or gangrene if we don't catch it.

"Of course I know," Patrick interjected, "Leper Island was my favorite reality show."

"Mom wasn't a fan," Mary told Patrick, "She thought it was degrading to lepers, but I liked it."

"Well, anyway," Fannie went on", Alec pre-arranged his proposal at a very fancy restaurant and afterwards I was so elated that when we got back in the car I let my hand dangle too close to the door when he closed it for me and it took my finger right off. I didn't even realize it. The whole ride home I'm thinking that I'm just light-headed from the proposal, when actually I was bleeding half to death. Neither one of us knew what had happened until Alec came around to let me out, and "plop," the finger just fell out on the ground."

"I'd still have that finger, if not for you." Fannie said, lovingly nudging Alec. A sheepish grin crossed Alec's face as he rolled his eyes toward his wife. "How romantic," Mary sighed.

"The two of you are so interesting." Patrick said, "but I really must be going. Maybe next time I'll get to meet your other charming daughter, Alice."

"If she's not too busy hanging around the bowling alley." Fannie mumbled under her breath.

"Now, mother, don't get started." Mary scolded. "Come on Patrick, I'll walk you to your car." She said, putting her pudgy arm through his.

Before Patrick drove off, they made plans to see each other the next day. Mary still didn't know much about Patrick. All he had told her was that he was a traveling salesman and was presently taking some time off to travel. Why a person with his obvious attributes would be working as a salesman was beyond her, and why a traveling salesman would take time off to "travel" seemed to make even less sense. "But," She told herself, "Why question fate?" Maybe she should have.

Chapter 2

Part Three
Harry Hears the News

Hulking Harry was picking up a carry-out dinner order at the back door of Norbin's Diner when he heard some women talking about Mary's more-interesting-than-thou new beau. He listened in disbelief. He was shocked and dismayed.

Not one guy in town had tried to approach Mary for at least six years, ever since her high school sweethearts, the Johnson Siamese Twins, Ty and Rone, had gotten killed in a fiery car crash on the treacherous "Crazy Snake Pass", an old unmaintained road that run through the hills south of Dipdrought.

A local female Rap artist, Heavy Floe, had gained international celebrity by writing a song about the incident called "Fiery Car Crash." Her debut album "Can't Stop the Floe" had gone multi-platinum and the single had gotten constant airplay. Poor Mary was tortured by the song for years. When she would least expect it, she would encounter it playing on a radio or on a music service or ringtone and break down in tears. Sometimes she would have nightmares about the crash and recite the song chorus in her sleep.

"What's easy to remember
is hard to forget
and she hasn't gotten over it yet
That fiery car crash is burned in her mind
That fiery car crash that burned them Aliiiive"

Then Mary would wake up screaming, which would wake the rest of her family and they would all go into her bedroom to console her. Mary's depression got so bad that she had to be committed to a mental hospital and stayed there for four years..

Harry had hoped that Mary might be so psychologically damaged that she would settle for someone like him, especially once he had perfected his invention and gotten rich. He then thought back to the first time he had seen her.

Mary was seventeen at the time, but already she had filled out very nicely. Harry was nineteen and was working the same job at Jawbone's he was still working at now, six years later, probably the only job he ever would have.

Jawbone's was sponsoring a pie-eating contest at the local Fourth of July Picnic. It was Harry's job to deliver the pies, then wait around and collect the empty pie tins after the event was over and return them to the bakery.

Harry watched in awe as Mary hoisted pie after pie and thrust them into her mouth, consuming each one in about four bites. The way that she hardly lost a crumb was art.

When the contest was over, Mary was the winner by almost two pies. When she rose to accept her one-hundred-dollar prize, she passed gas and let out a long, deep, belch at the same time. "Well." She remarked, "I guess that makes room for a little more." With that comment, she shoved another half of a pie down her gullet.

The audience went wild. They loved her, but not half as much as Harry did. "If only I could win her heart," He thought.

Now, after hearing the news about Mary's new beau Harry was devastated. All of his dreams were melting, cascading into a pool of hopelessness. He went back to his apartment and tried to work on his invention, but it was no use, he couldn't concentrate. His pain from the thought that he might lose any chance of winning Mary was too great. He lashed out at his invention, knocking it from the kitchen table and smashing it on the floor. He didn't care anymore. The world would have to live without "the ultimate doorstopper". Still, Harry could not let this mysterious stranger take Mary away from him without a fight. He knew he would not be satisfied unless he made at least one try to win the girl that he secretly loved.

Chapter 3

Emitt Airhardt

Emitt Airhardt was a tall, broad-shouldered, physically imposing, and brilliant, inventor. He had wavy brown hair and angelic good looks. He was a visionary who had made billions of dollars in the food industry.

Emitt was now in his late thirties and at the top of his game, a game that he had, pretty much invented, and one that the rest of the food industry wanted to be in on with him.

Emitt had made his first stab at business immortality when he was just 19 yrs old. He had concocted a tasteless, non-toxic, edible adhesive that could bind any food item and would dissolve upon contact with saliva. Thus, "Stick Foods" was born.

Any food, could now be put on stick, from mashed potatoes and gravy to spaghetti with meat sauce and even soup and it would stay put until it was bitten into. It could be warmed in the microwave or conventional oven or on the grill and still hold together. Only saliva would dissolve this bonding agent.

Emitt was sure that people would appreciate, embrace and, eventually, come to demand the convenience of having all of their favorite foods available on a stick, and, as it turned out, he was right.

Unfortunately, though a brilliant inventor, Emitt was naïve when it came to business dealings and his formula and his company were stolen from him by a group of acne-ridden financial backers to whom he had foolishly shown his entire process. He trusted the pizza faces and had lost everything. It wouldn't happen again.

While the crooks, who stole his company, were getting rich, Emitt went back to the drawing board. His second effort was a near failed attempt at an irresistible snack food, which he managed to salvage through marketing savvy. The snack actually tasted pretty darn good, sweet and savory. The problems were the appearance and texture. It looked like hairy, green moldy chunks of lunch meat and had a mushy and hairy mouth feel.

Emmitt decided to try and sell the snack just as it was. He dubbed it "Moldies" and called his company "Hardt Edged Foods" He shot a commercial in his home, posted it across social media and bought some billboard advertising.

The commercial showed Emmit, dressed in a blue business suit, standing behind his dining room table. In front of him was a silver platter with a domed lid. Over the table hung the Hardt Edged logo suspended by wires from the ceiling. Emmit smiled into the camera and steadily, evenly and convincingly, pitched his product.

"Hi, I'm Emmit Gaston Airhardt for Hardt Edged foods." He added the "Gaston" to his name to give himself an air of class. "We here at Hardt Edged have been on a mission for the last several years. A mission to bring to you, the snacking public, the one thing that you want most in a snack food, and after years of research, in markets across the country, we are convinced that the one quality that people value most in a snack food is not appearance, it's not texture and it's not shape. It's simply, and unconditionally, nothing more, but also nothing less, than mouth-watering great taste.

So, in our quest, we may have sacrificed some texture, and we may have sacrificed some appearance, but, Emitt continued" as he reached over and lifted the lid from the platter. Emmit used the remote to zoom the camera in on his product, taking himself out of the frame. He, then, leaned his face into the frame and looked, first at the platter and then back at the camera. "Sure." He says, "I know what it looks like, but just wait until you taste it."

Emitt, as they say, was on his way. Not in a big way and by no means was he a threat or even a blip on the radar screen of the giant "Stick Food Corp", but something had been happening in society. Nothing that had to do, so much, with Emitt's new snack food, but everything that had to do with timing.

In the same way that styles go in and out of fashion. Society had, many years earlier, begun a shift away from what had long been considered to be the shallow values of traditional good looks and beauty and people were looking beyond these traits, trying to find new ways to define beauty and self-worth, but regardless of what people thought, new values were not actually being introduced, the same values were merely being applied differently. This new system would only serve to shift the balance of power and highlight the shallowness that society was attempting to overcome.

This was the perfect time for a product like Moldies. It was quickly accepted and sales were steady. This modest success gave Emitt the money he needed to invest toward his next idea. An idea that would set the food industry on it's head, an idea so utterly fantastic and revolutionary that Emitt would be one of the wealthiest men on the planet within months of it's launch. This time, however, no one else would ever have the secret. Emitt harbored a great deal of hatred toward the pizza faces who had stolen his first idea and toward society in general for snubs he had received because of his average looks. He intended to go to great lengths to insure that the pieces of his new puzzle could only be joined by him, and when he died his secret would die with him.

He would change the world while he was living and it would just have to change back after he was gone.

Chapter 4

Doctor Monte Pinprick

Patrick and Mary dated every night of the first week after the dance. Mary began to fantasize about waddling down the aisle next to Patrick and had already started to hint at this in their conversations.

Patrick ignored her hints, acting as if he hadn't heard them. He was still wondering if staying in this town was a wise thing for him to do. Even though he was thousands of miles from his home town and from Emitt Airhardt, he knew Emitt would never stop hunting for him, and would never relax until he was dead.

Patrick also wasn't sure that his new identity would hold up under the close scrutiny of being married. He had already had to dodge questions from Mary about why he didn't have any social media accounts " Especially with a face as interesting as yours." Mary would say. Maybe he should keep moving on and try to lose himself in some sprawling metropolis instead of in this backwoods town.

Dr.Monte Pinprick was another blond haired, classically good looking guy and his boring looks had made him the butt of jokes throughout his life, especially in medical school. There was just nothing that special about him. He was a cookie cutter image of millions of other uninteresting people, who had been born without features that made them unique.

Now, however all of that had changed. Now he was the more-interesting-than-thou, Patrick Hatrick, who Mary had dubbed her "Bag of Quarters".

Patrick aka Monte was elated with his new station in life and since he'd met Mary he didn't want things to change, but he had to think. Even if Mary were the most interesting piece of tail he had ever gotten it on with, was she worth getting killed over? "Maybe she is," he told himself. "Hell sixteen months ago, when I was still the ordinary, boring looking Dr. Monte Pinprick, a girl like her wouldn't have looked my way twice."

Patrick lay on the bed in his hotel room and thought about how, all of his life he had struggled against prejudice directed at him because of his appearance. He remembered being a child and dreaming about being special. Nothing too drastic, maybe something like having one hand that was noticeably larger than the other, anything that would help him fit in with the favored crowd.

Some people who weren't born physically interesting, tried to fake a personality disorder, but that was a hard ruse to keep up 24/7. He thought back to a uninteresting looking gay classmate of his in medical school who had told people that he wasn't gay. He said the reason that he had sex with men, was because he had a rare affliction that prevented him from distinguishing between men and women.

Most of his acquaintances found it amusing and just went along with him. Some had nameplates made up that said "MAN" or "WOMAN" and would put them on when he came around.

Monte wasn't so lucky, for some reason people seemed to go out of their way to torture him. In medical school, his classmates, and even some thoughtless teachers were not above making crude remarks to him, like "How do you expect to get patients with those boring looks? Have you considered garbage collection, or delivery work instead?"

Monte could count all of his true, interesting looking friends in his life on one hand. Actually he could count them on one finger, since there was only one, and that one was his friend-to-the-end, Dr. Erin Judgement.

Dr. Judgement was a bug-eyed, Malaysian Dwarf, who he had met during his internship at Mt Heinie

Hospital. She was the head of Plastic Surgery. She was well liked and highly respected. She had taken a liking to the young Dr. Pinprick upon meeting him and did what she could to keep his interesting looking colleagues from making his job any harder than it was already.

Monte owed here for that, and for much, much more. More than he could ever repay. Most of all he owed her for his new identity.

She had, bravely, put at risk everything she had worked her entire for to just to come to his aid. Her good reputation and medical license would both be history if anyone ever found out about the secret operation that had changed the boring Dr. Monte Pinprick, able Rectal Surgeon, into the more-interesting-than-thou, Patrick Hatrick, world-class heartthrob.

It was an ultimate sacrifice. A sacrifice she had made without even knowing the details of his dilemma. She was defying the biggest taboo there was, but she did it without reservation after she found him in his office on the verge of a breakdown.

He was babbling about people wanting to kill him while nervously walking around his office collecting things and putting them in a suitcase. She knew her friend was in serious trouble. She didn't ask who he thought was going to kill him, or even why. All she knew was that he needed help, and that was enough for her. "Would a new identity help?" she asked.

Monte stopped and looked at his friend. One of the most skilled and respected plastic surgeons in the country was making him an offer that could destroy her career. How could he even ask her to do what she was suggesting? How could he ask her to risk so much for him?

"Yes." He replied in a desperate voice.

"I guess it really wasn't that hard." He thought to himself.

Dr. Judgment took a good look at Monte's face and head. "Operating room "B," she told him, "give me about fifteen minutes. I have to get a bat, an ice pick and a meat tenderizer".

Maybe Dr. Judgement should have asked what the hell was going on with Monte. Maybe then she would have understood why two thugs were waiting for her when she came home one night. Why they beat her black and blue and bounced her off of the walls, all the while demanding to know where Monte was. "We know you must know." They told her. "It's no secret that you were his only friend."

Even through this hellish ordeal she did not betray Monte. Not intentionally, anyway. The thugs did, however, while ransacking her house, come across a major clue. They found before and after pictures from the face altering operation she had performed on Monte. His face was still swollen when the pictures were taken, but they were good enough.

"So, you don't know anything, do you?" one of the thugs said, turning his attention back to Dr. Judgement as she lay in a ball on floor. He walked over and picked her up. Her pathetically small frame dangling from his hugely muscled arms. "Now, tell us where to find him." He demanded, shaking her violently. But she was just hung there, limp and unresponsive. He let her go and she dropped with a thud, lifelessly to the floor.

It didn't matter, they had what they needed. It was just a matter of time now

Chapter 5

The Invention

Emitt Airhardt needed inspiration. His first invention was, now, making other people wealthy. How could he even hope to match its success? The answer would come, as inspired ideas always do, suddenly and unexpectedly.

Emitt was walking to his car one evening, cell phone in hand, calling ahead for Chinese carry-out when he remembered something, something that had occurred during the development of the bonding material for his food-on-a-stick invention. He recalled how, after binding the food with an earlier version of his adhesive it had turned to very small amount of liquid when it was vacuum sealed and then into a lumpy mess when he reopened the package.

What if, he thought, he could make some adjustments to this formula, if he could still have the food reduce to a small amount of liquid when it was sealed, but then, it would restore to its original state when the package was opened?

He went to back to his notes and began experimenting. Emitt's mind went on auto-pilot. The rate at which he could process information was amazing, it had always been the one thing that gave him the greatest thrill. He could juggle hundreds of bits of information and never lose track. Once he was focused toward a goal he would not quit until he had exhausted every avenue he could fathom, every scenario he could conjure up. While he was experimenting on one possible solution, he was already thinking ten steps ahead to future ones.

In this case, it didn't take him long. He had his desired results within 18 mos. He now could reduce any type of food, fresh or prepared, into a liquid a fraction of it's original size by spraying it with his solution and then removing the air with a vacuum seal. A ten pound pot roast, for example would be reduced to approximately one half cup of liquid. When air was reintroduced the food would regenerate to its original state.

Now Emitt faced another problem. How to package his product! He didn't want the liquid analyzed by competitors. He needed a package that would not allow the liquid to be extracted without introducing air. He needed a package that would split, or break open if it was tampered with at all. He needed packaging that could only be opened by the method that he would build into it. The packaging was as vital as the formula itself.

Nearly another year went by before Emitt had solved this problem, but when he did, the result was quite exceptional in look as well as in performance. The material was paper thin with an fragile eggshell like feel, but was nearly indestructible.The packaging could be made in various sizes and colors. The first one was like a small spray bottle with a removeable cap. Beneath the cap was a button. When this button was pushed, the other end of the container would fracture, releasing its contents. Later on the larger containers would have other opening devices, each of them with a method for introducing air into the liquid a fraction of a second before it completely opened. Even if in a vacuum.

The casing was made in two layers. Between these layers was a microfilm of millions to billions of oxygen molecules. Violating the outer layer would cause the inner layer to fracture, releasing the oxygen into the liquid and start the restoration process.

As far as the container assembly and the production of the spray went, only Emitt would know the proper calibrations and formula. Once the machines were assembled, the process would be closed. He would control all of the programming while laborers performed any physical tasks that were required.

Emitt contacted the FDA, their tests took almost another three years, but the process was finally given their stamp of approval, even though Emitt never allowed them to actually analyze his formula and it took a fair amount of "um" donations to accomplish that.

Emitt was now able to begin demonstrating to food producers how he could ship their products at a fraction of the cost they were presently incurring. His method, required no refrigeration for fresh meats or produce and had an indefinite shelf life. He showed them how any type of food could be conveniently transported in his containers, and how full meals could be made at the push of a button. He allowed their experts to examine the before and after results.

Prepared foods could now be enjoyed with a convenience that not even the food-on-a-stick people could offer and one semi-trailer or train car could transport hundreds or thousands of times the amount of product that they used to in one shipment. Orders trickled in for a few months, then overnight, exploded.

Emitt had reinvented the tin can far beyond anyone's wildest imagination.

Chapter 6

Airhardt meets Pinprick

Emitt Airhardt was blessed with a brilliant mind, and now his formidable wealth commanded respect, at least to his face. Still, he was all too aware that his uninteresting, predictably boring features were responsible for numerous social snubs he had received during his rise, and even now to a lesser extent.

In his mind he needed further validation that his success was preordained. He also wanted his children to taste the one fruit of life that was denied to him, interesting looks.

Emitt's wife, Chunky, had recently become pregnant and he was praying that their child would inherit some of his wife's interesting traits. Be it her droopy eyelids, exaggerated saddlebag legs or her small pinhead. Then, as so often happens, fate, or coincidence, if you will, stepped in.

Emitt was in need of a hemorrhoid operation and his primary physician referred him to Dr. Monte Pinprick.

In Monte, Emitt saw a kindred spirit. A successful man who had to endure the same prejudices that Emitt had. Emitt decided to make the young doctor Pinprick a bold offer.

On the pretense of needing immediate medical care, Emitt summoned Monte to his mansion, but once Monte arrived, Emitt pitched him his plan.

Emitt asked Monte if he would like to be financially set for life. Time being of the essence, he made Monte a point blank offer. Would he take ten million dollars to alter the genes of Emitt's unborn child while in the womb, to guarantee that it would be born with interesting features.

"I'm sure that your child will be born with interesting looks without any interference from me" Monte, nervously, told Emitt, wanting, at that moment, to be anywhere else than where he was. Monte couldn't believe that he was being asked to do something so taboo. He knew that there were schlock doctors who performed teratoid operations in motels and shady backroom clinics, but for a physician of Monte's professional background to be asked to do such a thing was unthinkable. The price, however, was right.

The two men locked eyes and shook hands. "No one will ever know." Emitt said firmly. "How soon can it be done?"

"Not so fast." Monte countered, "I want half of the money up front and in cash. The other half, immediately after your wife delivers."

"I have that much in my safe. I can get it for you now." Emitt told him.

"Where is your wife now?" Monte asked.

"She's upstairs, sleeping." Emitt answered.

"Get the money." Monte replied. "I have to return to my office for a few more implements".

When Monte came back Emitt handed him a satchel. Monte glanced in it and nodded. Emitt led him to the bedroom where Chunky lay fast asleep. "I already gave her a sleeping pill", Emitt told him, "Okay, maybe more than one", he admitted.

Monte acknowledged Emitt's admission with a nod, then asked him to go back downstairs. Monte would call him when he was through.

"Wait," Emitt said, "There is one more thing." Emitt produced a vial, which he handed to Monte. The two men discussed the contents of the vial for a minute, then Emitt left.
About fifteen minutes later, Monte was finished. Emitt was surprised to see him coming down the staircase so soon.

"You're finished already?" Emitt asked suspiciously.

"Sure." Monte answered, "Back in medical school we did this with fruit flies all the time."

Emitt was not convinced. "You did everything I requested?"

"Everything!" Monte said. He took the now empty vial that Emitt had given him earlier, from his jacket pocket and returned it to him.

Emitt held up the vial and examined it.

"Don't worry." Monte said with a smile and a surgeon's reassuring manner. "Everything will be O.K.

Monte picked up his satchel of cash and headed out the door. He was already having second thoughts. He knew everything was not going to be O.K. Not for him anyway. He was sure that in spite of his deal with Airhardt, that Emitt could not afford to let him live. There was too much for him to lose if people found out what Monte had done for him. He was sure that if he stuck around that his days would be numbered, and these instincts would prove to be correct.

The money that Emitt paid to Monte was never intended to be a down payment on their deal. It had always been intended to be payment for the men who would come to kill the doctor, and it had to be done quickly. Emitt could not take the chance that Monte might try to confide in someone else what had transpired that night.

As many powerful people do, Emitt knew people who could handle these types of delicate situations. Well, at least, he knew people, who knew people, who knew people, who knew of people, who knew people who could handle these types of situations. Everything had been prearranged. Emitt took out his phone and texted a message. The text failed, "message not delivered." He tried again. The text failed again. "Dammit." He thought, "Oh well I'll just do it in the morning." He grumbled, then he went to bed.

Monte hurried to his apartment and began packing. He would vanish, no one would ever find him. He had enough money to start over somewhere else. "Stupid." He thought to himself, "Stupid, stupid, stupid." He was already wishing that this entire night had never happened.

He loaded up his car and headed to his office at the hospital to retrieve the rest of his things.

Chapter 7

Harry and Patrick

Patrick was spending the evening at Mary's house. Mary's parents were out for the night and Mary wanted to impress Patrick with her cooking skills. Patrick sat in the living room watching TV while Mary bounced around the kitchen preparing food, humming and smiling as she went along.

Outside a thunderstorm was brewing and rain had begun to fall. Down the street, parked by the curb, Hulking Harry sat in his tiny, blue Ford Hovel, his eyes fixed on Patrick's rented big, white, Buick Grand Monarch which was parked in front of Mary's house. Harry was waiting for Patrick to leave. He planned to follow and confront him. He was sure something was not right with this mysterious stranger and he was determined to, either find out what it was, or if he was wrong, succeed in looking like a complete fool. It didn't really matter at this point. Harry was too distressed and too depressed to think straight. These were the actions of a desperate man in an impossible situation who didn't know what else to do.

The fact that Mary didn't even know who he was, was completely lost on him, poor guy.

Harry sat for nearly five hours, watching Mary's house. He imagined himself inside with her, just as he had imagined numerous times before. Harry saw her round, squat frame cuddling next to him on the couch, her pudgy feet sticking out over the side.

 Harry closed his eyes and embraced the steering wheel as if it were Mary. Without thinking, he squeezed against it until a sudden blast from the horn blew apart the fabric of his dream like a hard sneeze through tissue paper. Startled, Harry ducked down under the dashboard and hoped no one would come to investigate. No one did.

 Minutes passed before Harry finally peeked back up over the dashboard, and when he did he saw Mary, standing on the front porch, kissing Patrick goodnight. He watched Patrick get into his rented Grand Monarch and drive away. Harry followed in his Hovel.

Harry was surprised when Patrick did not head back towards the downtown area, but instead seemed to be heading out of town, and not just out of town. He was headed south on Dense road, and the only place that Dense road led to was the treacherous Crazy Snake Pass. The same pass where the Johnson twins had crashed and burned years earlier. "Only a fool would take the "Snake" at night." Harry thought, "and only a suicidal fool would take it in the rain." Patrick, now, knew one thing for certain. "This guy is definitely not from these parts."

Crazy Snake was a shortcut through the mountains south of Dipdrought. Two narrow lanes of well-worn blacktop meandering through a series of ten rises, eight of which sloped into treacherous curves. There were no roadside reflectors or road signs along the, roughly, four mile stretch of road. There were only two signs, one posted at each end of the pass, that read "Are You Sure You Want to do this?"

What Harry didn't know was that Patrick was on his way out of town for good. He had decided not to stay in Dipdrought after all. His hotel bill was paid two weeks ahead so the hotel would think that he was still there. He left taking only the money he had with him, some of his clothes and few toiletries. The only reason that he was taking the pass was because he needed to pick up the rest of his money. Patrick had hidden out in these woods while his surgical scars healed. He had secreted over four million dollars near his campsite and had to collect it before leaving. He had driven the pass several times before and was sure that he could negotiate it with no problem.

Patrick looked in his rearview mirror and saw another car behind him. He slowed to see if the other car would speed up and pass him, but it also slowed. "Someone is following me. What if Airhardt has found me?" he thought. Patrick began to panic, then calmed himself. "There is no way they can keep up with me once we reach the pass. I'll lose them for sure." Patrick eased the gas peddle towards the floorboard and accelerated toward the pass.

The rain was steadily coming down and the wheels on Harry's Hovel were bald, but he wasn't about to turn back. He sped up after the Monarch.

Patrick kept checking his rearview mirror and was becoming increasingly concerned about the car behind him. The distraction almost made him skid off the road at one point. He decided that he would not go back to his campsite, instead he would continue to the highway and drive as far it took to shake the other car. He would come back later for his money.

Patrick was taking it slow and counting the curves. After a nerve racking 30 or so minutes he knew he was coming to the last rise, over which was the straight road to the main highway so he gunned it. He hit the top of the rise going so fast that his car flew a couple of inches off of the pavement.

There are a number of words that could describe how Patrick felt when he realized that he had miscounted the rises. Horrified, shocked and terrified are a few. "I want my mommy", is another, when he found himself headed into a 20 mph turn traveling at about 80 miles per hour.

He hit the brakes while still airborne and came down hard on the blacktop. His car went spinning into the curve like a pinwheel. Harry followed suit and ended up in the same predicament.
Round and round they spun, like two cars on a Tilt-a-Whirl track, until they both flew off onto opposite sides of the road, each car hitting a tree, bursting into flames and ejecting its occupant.

Patrick landed by Harry's car and Harry, somehow landed inside of Patrick's burning car. Harry was the only survivor.

Harry awoke in the hospital, days later, his head and face wrapped in bandages and an excited Mary was standing over him. "Thank God, Patrick, that you finally woke up. The doctors said it was a miracle that you even survived. If the rain hadn't dampened the fire you might have been burned ali…. Mary choked on the last word suddenly overcome with emotion at the memory of Ty and Rone"

It didn't take Patrick long to figure out what had happened. He was being mistaken for the Bag of Quarters, somehow they had gotten them mixed up at the hospital, but he was sure that when the bandages came off him and the other driver that they would realize their mistake. "So what about the other driver"? he asked Mary.

"Oh, him? There was nobody in the other car, only drag marks and paw prints around it. Looks like bears or something got him, but who cares? The important thing is that you're alive".

"Wow", Harry thought, "maybe I can pull this off after all. I can feign amnesia about anything I'm not sure of and Mary will finally be mine".

After weeks of waiting the day arrived when Harry's surgeon announced it was time to remove the bandages for good, but he didn't come to the room alone. Virtually every doctor and nurse in the hospital came to see the results.

Harry took measured breaths to control his nervousness. Not a sound was made as the dressing was unwrapped. When the doctor was finished he held up a mirror for Harry to see himself. Harry was dumbfounded, he was no longer boring Harry. He now was Patrick. The doctors had reconstructed his face to resemble the "Bag of Quarters," the person who they thought he was and, he now, even had interesting burn scars about his face and body.

A cheer went up in the room. Congratulations were passed around and then someone went out into the hall to get Mary. She had been too nervous to come in for the ungauzing, but now she stood there beaming with adoration. It was all the dreams Harry had ever had in his entire life coming true at the same moment. It was overwhelming. He was speechless. His head was swimming.

"I think we'll leave the two of you alone." The head surgeon said, turning to Mary. The staff began to file out of the room, each one casting backward glances at Harry. He heard words being muttered, like "amazing", "unbelievable", "luckiest man in the world." Harry couldn't have agreed more.

Mary went up to the hospital bed and fell forward into Harry's arms. "My darling, my darling." She said over and over.

Harry didn't know what was softer, Mary's skin or the blubber underneath. Oh, and that smell! What was that smell? Then it struck him, it was that smell that comes off your belly button lint. "It's all those rolls of fat." He thought. "I guess it's not possible to get them all clean all of the time." What an unexpected bonus."

Harry told himself that all he had to do now was just go along for the ride. He was sure that from here on in only good things would happen for him.

"Come on." Mary said. "Let's get you checked out of here and go to your hotel so I can show you how happy I am to have you back. I brought some clothes that were hanging up in your room, because the ones you were wearing were all burned up and so was your wallet with your melted IDs inside. We couldn't find your key card on you but the hotel was gracious enough to let me in, considering the circumstances. Turns out you're so absent minded that you left it in the desk drawer."

On the way out of the hospital, several nurses giggled and smiled at Harry. On the street he caught more women giving him appreciative glances. By the time he and Mary had finished celebrating at the Coat and Arms, he had come to an unexpected change of mind. Looking at Mary he thought, "Heck, I can do better than her", barely even paying attention as she exited the room. "I'll be back around sevenish." Mary called out to Harry, but he just turned and walked into the bathroom without even responding.

Once Mary was gone Harry began going through Patrick's room looking for personal information. He went through the dresser drawers, under the bed and through the closet. In the closet he found a charred, blue leather suitcase. Obviously it had been in Patrick's car at the time of the accident. When he picked it up it was apparent someone had already forced it open. Inside he found some clothes and toiletries, no documents or other clues to Patrick's identity, or so it appeared at first glance.

Harry, for some reason didn't think the suitcase looked quite right. The inside looked ok but there seemed to be a little more to one side of the case than was necessary. He probed around the outer seam with his fingers, then began to pull. He heard the sound of Velcro as a false bottom came free. Inside he found money. A lot of money, along with a piece of paper and some IDs of an extremely boring looking man named Monte. On the paper a map was scribbled. Harry recognized the area. It was a backwoods location beyond the fifth southbound curve of "Crazy Snake Pass."

Harry phoned the front desk for a rental car. He wanted to find out what was out there. He still had a few hours of daylight and didn't want to wait. He packed the clothes back into the suitcase and stuffed as much money as he could into his pockets. He was just about to leave when he was startled by a knock at the door.

"Housekeeping, Mr. Hatrick, can we come in and clean your room?"

"Sure, come on in, I was just going out anyway."

Chapter 8

Daddyhood, Emitts Change of Heart

Becoming a parent changes people, there are of course exceptions, Emitt was not one of these exceptions. The birth of his child brought profound changes to his way of thinking, it had been one of those "good news", "bad news", "ambivalent news" situations.

Emitt, now back at his mansion, sat down in his living room and turned on his Bang & Olafson 3D Surreal Holographic TV. The TVs projection device was mounted in the floor and projected the 3D images of the movie on a platform in the middle of room. He turned the size adjustment to 1/8 of actual size and watched a scene from one of his favorite action movies. He poured himself a shot of 1921 Tequila and sipped at it, savoring the taste, rolling it around in his mouth before swallowing.

Quite a lot had happened during the last several months. Events that Emitt had never, ever envisioned and only now was much of it beginning to congeal in his mind. He was like the man who looked at his wife on her fortieth birthday and told her how he'd always been aware that at forty she wouldn't look the same as she had at twenty. "I knew you'd have some grey hairs. I knew your skin would begin to sag and that you'd probably have put on some pounds, but until this moment I just never really put it all together." Originally told as a joke, it had, since, become a serious toast.

Emitt thought about the road that had led society to the present state of affairs. The "Civil Rights" movement, the "Gay Rights" movement. All of the political correctness in and out of the workplace. The weight, height, handicapped and age anti-discrimination laws. Yes, good intentions aimed at creating an accepting and forward thinking environment in which all people, no matter how different or disadvantaged could enjoy lives unhindered by the prejudices and disapproval of others. In fact the goal had been to eradicate prejudice and unfair treatment of anyone's inherent or unfortunate state of being.

Bold, unprecedented steps were taken toward this end. So many disenfranchised groups were included in new affirmative action policies, that very few people outside of these guidelines could even find employment. Eventually the status quo shifted to where you almost needed to have a physical abnormality to find a decent paying job. This led to an eventual and dramatic shift of power, political and corporate.

Government contracts and grants were influenced by these policies and as a direct result, deformed faces had began showing up in boardrooms and workplaces across the country. New groups of people came into wealth and power. There was the Lobster People Dynasty and the Elephant People and Progeria Conglomerates among others.

Emitt remembered the businessmen who had installed Mongoloids as puppet figureheads. They hoped that the Mongoloid's presence would improve their companies standing in the business community while enabling them to maintain complete control. What a disaster that had turned into. The ruse was so transparent that the company was shamed out of business.

It seemed that everybody and their in-bred cousins were lobbying for special favor. It had gotten so ridiculous that the government had to tighten up their guidelines to exclude people with more common traits like long necks, big noses, moles, acne...etc.

All of these good intentions had accomplished nothing. Well nothing of substance, nothing of value. The only difference now was that opposite groups of people were espousing that we were all the same on the inside and that appearance and preferences weren't important. That was ridiculous, because the last thing we all are is the same on the inside, that's why we need laws in the first place.

Emitt decided that he had had enough. He regretted what he had done to his child. His "child" was all he could call it. At this point no one was sure if it even had a gender. Dr. Pinprick had succeeded impressively. That was the "good news" that now had become the "bad news". The "ambivalent news" was that Emitt's wife, Chunky, had died during childbirth.

Emitt thought about the beverage line he had started so that his child could inherit it when he grew up. The potato juice cocktail had been the first product and it was a huge success.Now he was disgusted with himself. As brilliant and successful as he was, he had allowed himself to be manipulated by the ill-formed opinions of others. All that this change in society had proven is what everyone already knew. Nobody wants equality, everybody just wants supremacy and if that was the name of the game then he had already proven that he was a supreme being.

It was time for this aberrant condition to end. Emitt did not begrudge anyone a legitimate claim to success, but he would no longer be a party to this moral guilt trip.

Paraphrasing, Emitt recalled a quote he had once read. Something about how people's weaknesses so often override what they consider to be their strengths. Sometimes that line is blurred. Even now, as he sat and thought about the changes he intended to make, he wasn't absolutely sure that he wasn't giving into his weaknesses. Was he merely considering acts of retaliation or was he really looking to right what he saw to be wrongs? One situation on his mind was a little of both. He was thinking about the vial he had given to Dr. Pinprick on the night that he had operated on Chunky.

The vial contained the DNA of all three of the pizza faces who had stolen his food-on-a-stick formula, it was easy to get. During their time together a great many stains had been left on Emitt's furniture from their oozing pimples. He cut out swatches and stored them in vacuum sealed containers after they double-crossed him. He hoped he could somehow, eventually use the DNA to get revenge on them and that move had turned out to be a brilliant one. He was right and the time had finally come. They betrayed his trust and now he was going to return the favor.

Originally the DNA was introduced into Emitt's child's embryo as insurance, in case Dr. Pinprick had not delivered on his promise and his child was born without any interesting traits. Emitt would demand a DNA test be performed and then disown the baby when the foreign DNA was discovered. He would accuse his wife of cheating on him and getting pregnant during a gang bang with his acne ravaged enemies whose business fortunes had already been diminishing every year. He would divorce her, be rid of her and the child and get an added measure of revenge at the same time. Now he still would use the ploy to rid himself of the child, but for the opposite reason.

The lawyers would work it out. As far as he was concerned it was a dead issue. That problem dealt with Emitt could turn his attention toward more important matters like changes he intended to make at his company, starting with the spokespersons. He would look for product representatives with classical good looks to replace his current line-up of disfigured and disabled models. He had grown tired of seeing the smug looks on their faces anyway. He also intended to replace all of the moving handicapped ramps at his factories and office bldgs with stationary ones. After that he would begin looking at what changes he wanted to make to his corporate line-up. Time to start putting people back in their places.

It was ironic how the situation had come to this point. If Emitt's first invention hadn't been stolen he may never have gone on to his greater invention and none of this would even be happening. Maybe he should be thankful instead of hateful. Maybe he would serve as a much better example of humanity if he didn't seek revenge. Maybe he should, instead try to show people how the world would be a much better place if everyone just put aside their differences and pretended to get along. Oh well, so much for fairy tales, now back to reality.

A chilly breeze began blowing into the living room through the open French doors on the patio. Emitt got up to close them. He crossed the room and walked through the holographic movie scene that was playing out on the floor. He paused for moment and looked down at the miniature figures running around at his feet, shooting at each other. "Cool," He said aloud, momentarily distracted from his other thoughts.

Emitt closed the doors, then returned to his chair. Yes, he had a lot of thinking to do, he took another sip of the 1921 tequila then laid back comfortably in his easy chair. More comfortably than he had in quite a while.

Mary, Mary
Quite Inconsolable

The Final Chapter

"A bag of quarters! A bag of quarters!" Mary called out, her cries issuing through the halls of the Oregon State Mental Hospital.

"There she goes again." Nurse Klein said, shaking her head. Nurse Polk glanced up from her paperwork, "yeah, I think she's definitely lost it for good. You want to give her a sedative or should I?"

"I'll give it to her," nurse Klein answered, "but, you know, try to put yourself in her place. How do you think you would be if everything that happened to her happened to you? First of all, she's not even anything special or unique, she's just a common roly-poly, but somehow the most interesting men keep falling for her, like the Johnson twins in high school, but what happens? They die in a fiery car crash".

"Ladies, ladies". It was the Hospital Administrator, Dr. Dolores Mitchel hastily approaching the nurses station. "Ladies I need your attention. We will be hosting a very distinguished guest this afternoon and I need both of you to be completely professional when she gets here. Heavy Floe is coming to observe and talk to Mary, so hopefully you haven't had to sedate her tonight."

"We were just about to," Nurse Klein said, "you caught us just in time."

"Good," Dr. Mitchel said, because Floe is researching "Fiery Car Crash Too", the follow-up to her first hit single "Fiery Car Crash", and, "Head Nurse Mitchell added, " I hear she's bringing her opening act with her."

"You mean those lesbian twins, the "Clone Dykes?" God, I can't stand them and that stupid message song of theirs, "Take a Minute of Your Day." makes me want to vomit." nurse Klein said.

"Me too." Nurse Polk chimed in." Take a minute of your day, don't look the other way. Take a minute of your day, don't look the other way." she went on, mocking the song. "Yeah, take a minute out of your day to recognize other people's problems, sure, we all know that they're really just concerned with gay issues. They don't really give a shit about anybody else. Nobody's taking minute out their day to do anything for us and our boring lives"

The "Clone Dykes" song had been prompted by the comment that their father made when they "came out" to him. "Really? You made me take a minute out of my day for that? Is it okay it I get back to my tv show now?" He had responded.

The girls looked at each other in a moment of shared inspiration. "Yeah, they said, everyone should take at least a minute out of their day to recognize the plights of others. Thanks dad," and off to their room they went to write the song, which became a modest hit."

"Look." Dr. Mitchell, went on, "You may not like them now, but I know how these things go. You might feel a lot different after meeting the Dykes in person, but no matter how star struck you are, I don't want either one of you asking anyone for their autograph or bothering them in any way. Now, Heavy will probably have some questions for the two of you. Just answer whatever she asks, and that's all. Do not try making chit chat. Do you understand ? "

"Yes Ma'am." They answered.

Dr Mitchel then softened her demeanor and reached into her purse. "Here, these are for you," she said, producing a couple of autographed pink ipods that looked like Tampon cases, Tampon being the sponsor of Heavy Floe's tour. "These are autographed prototypes of Floe's new album

"Heavier than Ever" which is now going to be called "Fiery Car Crash Too" with some exclusive sample tracks on them that won't appear on the new album. No one outside of her inner circle has these. When her manager called to set up the interview, he offered me "one" to butter me up, but I told him that we would need "three". Dr. Mitchel said, smiling.

"Thank you, Ma'am." The girls said excitedly.

"O.K., now you ladies have a good evening, and don't forget what I said." Dr. Mitchel told them, then she headed back to her office.

Nurse Klein looked at nurse Polk, "Can you believe this?" she asked.

"Wow." Nurse Polk said, "You know, Dr. Mitchel is alright. She doesn't let that goiter go to her head."

"She sure doesn't." Nurse Klien answered. "I wonder if this album is going to be as good as "Can't Stop the Floe?"

"I Pull My Own Strings" was my favorite," Nurse Polk said. "Still Floe'in" was a little weak, but it had some good stuff on it. I still, can't believe this. I love "Heavy". She's so real. I saw her story on "Fuse." She never forgot her roots, she's still just a regular person. I'm sure she wouldn't care if we asked her a few questions or took a selfie."

"Well, I don't know about that, I don't want to risk losing my job, but anyway, as I was saying," nurse Klien went on, and at that same moment, Mary began screaming again from her room.

Nurse Klien waited a few moments for Mary to stop, then finished her thought. "Suppose everything that happened to Mary had happened to you. Her first loves die in a fiery car crash and she's sure that she's lost her one chance at happiness and then what happens, a hit song is written about the crash and she's constantly reminded of the tragedy. For years she's tortured by this song. Then finally it dies down and she manages to get her head back together and go on with her life."

"I know," nurse Polk interjects, "and then what happens, her life starts looking up again when the most interesting man to pass through Dipdrought in years, for some unfathomable reason, falls for her, and then what happens to him? He gets into a fiery car crash in the same place where her first loves crashed, burned and died."

"But", nurse Klein says taking over, "he doesn't die. Instead, miraculously, he lives and the doctors reconstruct his face to an even more interesting condition than it was before the accident and now his body even has interesting burn scars. I mean the situation just keeps getting better and better, but then, what happens?"

"Exactly", nurse Polk says, "then, this guy, Mary's second true love, is found dead in his hotel room, shot through the head several times and nobody knows why. Heck, nobody even knows who this guy really was."

"And now," nurse Klein says, "Heavy Floe is writing Fiery Car Crash Too, and you know that song is going to be a hit, maybe even a bigger hit than the first song."

"Right," nurse Polk said, "and for sure the radio and all the music channels will be bringing back the original song and the video as well, not to mention all of the people who will probably download the new one for a ring tone. Not only that, but you know someone will definitely make Mary's story into a movie. She'll be haunted by this for the rest of her life."

"So, I ask you," nurse Klein says, "what if all of that had happened to you? How do you think you would be at this point?"

"You know how I'd be," nurse Polk said, "I'd be thinking, boy, does someone up there like me or what? What an interesting life I'm having!"

"You know it," nurse Klein answered, "I'd be looking at the other girls like, "What do you mean you never had even one man get blown up over you? Heck, I've had three, and one of them was blown up <u>and</u>

shot nine times. You girls aren't even in my class, don't even bother talking to me.

The two nurses laughed for a minute, then nurse Klein went on. "Instead, she's in there crying, and going crazy and everything. That phony roly-poly. Gland problem, my foot. I could be like her too if I didn't have any self-respect. Just stuff my face full of food all day and claim that it's a medical condition. I'd give my right eye to be in her position."

Nurse Polk gave nurse Klein a concerned look.

"Oh, don't worry," nurse Klein said, I'm not going to do anything drastic. All that I'm saying is that I wish I could have something special like that happen in my life."

"Yeah, me too." Nurse Polk answered. "I guess some people just don't know how to appreciate what they've got."

THE END

Made in the USA
Monee, IL
07 February 2021